DELICATES

For anyone who feels lost, hurt, or alone.
You matter.

DELICATES

Brenna Thummler

AN ONI PRESS PUBLICATION

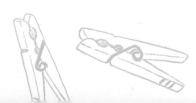

Okay, I see the ice cream cone.

squeeze

Come on, Wendell.

There are only two days left of summer. You've been stuck there since last fall.

How do **you** know?

You spent most of it with **Col·ton.**

That's not true.

I bet **he's** a **great** swimmer now.

It's a friend group, not just Colton.

Are you boyfriend and girlfriend?

What? NO!

Come on, Marjorie. There are two days left of summer, and you've been stuck **here** since last fall.

9

...too bad...sun's rising, so it's time for you to sleep.

Who were you talking to?

Oh... uh...what?

I'm usually out here all alone this early.

But I don't talk to myself.

What are you doing?

This is the best time for ghosts, I think.

See here?

This is Lorraine.

tap tap

Like Lorraine Warren.

Anyway, I'm working on a whole ghost collection. You know, for my portfolio.

Oh, uh. Wow.

So, you were talking to yourself?

I guess so.

That's weird.

Yeah, well, tell that to Lorraine.

See ya.

NOW OPEN THROUGH OCTOBER

NOW OPEN THROUGH OCTOBER

flop

Marj—your friends are here!

Marjie May!

Hey.

Okay, here's how it went: The few sorta-dates with my non-boyfriend, Colton, were weird. I was weird. I don't understand how people can find boyfriends comforting.

I thought a friend group might fix the problem, and then this just sort of happened. I mean, he had a group to offer, and all of my friends are in a laundry basket.

Grab your towel and let's go!

I should probably check on the laundry—

No, no! Go! I've got it covered.

Don't you have that quilt charity meeting today?

Oh...is that today?

I, uh...I'll probably just wait and go next week.

Go!

Go have fun with your friends.

Hearing that they're my "friends" still feels...wrong?

I guess that's expected when your former nemesis now refers to you as "Marjie May" and bought you matching chokers.

Maybe she's trying to strangle me.

But I'll admit, it feels good to fit in somewhere.

mmm

Aw, yeah, the sticks.

DROP IT, SID.

Who knows when I'll eat normal food again.

Sorry, I forgot about Trudy Booty Camp.

My mom's a vegetarian.

Wow, Sasha, your life is so hard.

Tessi's mom is nuts.

Yeah, well, you know: "Carbs might lure the devil."

But I can take him.

We really have to get you a bikini.

There's your headline:

"Local youth spend summer's end at pool, avoid all contact with water."

Hey, there are some puddles in my driveway. Why pay to come here when you can sit around those for free?

Do you have mozzarella sticks?

Let's see...I have carrot sticks.

Sticks of butter.

Ew.

Aren't teachers supposed to have summers off?

Not married ones.

My wife told me to spend the summer break saving lives.

The "Superman" position was filled, so here I am.

So, eighth grade, huh? Top of the social ladder?

We were always at the top, Duncan Donut.

Except for this one, here.

But we're fixing that.

And how about you, Cheshire Glatt?

Feeling good about this year?

Yeah, I think so.

Do you guys know my oldest daughter, Eliza?

Two arms, all ten fingers I think, had toast for breakfast?

Oh, Eliza. Yeah. We *love* Eliza.

She's actually going to be in your class this year.

Wasn't she in eighth grade last year?

Mmm. Darn girl wouldn't eat her peas, and we had to punish her somehow.

We considered locking her in a tower somewhere, but eighth grade is essentially the same.

Oh, I'm sure you'll make it out okay.

Wait, she's getting held back?

Yeah... yeah.

She wasn't quite ready to move to the high school.

Eliza's crazy smart, which she got from me, obviously.

She, uh, has trouble focusing... she's strong-willed, you know?

Likes to go her own way rather than listen to other people.

That she got from my brother-in-law.

Well, don't you worry, Mr. Duncan. We'll look out for her.

Hey, I appreciate it.

Good to finally be free of *that* fatherly obligation.

Ha, you're funny, Mr. Duncan.

All right, I'll catch all you hooligans next week.

Enjoy the concrete.

Later, Mr. Duncan.

Bye!

See ya.

Eliza—is that the girl with the fancy camera?

Ugh, **yes.** She's such a freak.

Oh. I thought—

Darcie caught her sneaking around her house after dark last year,

28

taking pictures like it was totally normal.

That is, um...weird.

And do you know she believes in *ghosts?!*

Like, honest to God, thinks they're real and wants to photograph them.

Ghosts.

We *should* look out for her—

she might get possessed.

Hey, I totally believe in ghosts.

What is he talking about?

See, there's one now.

Oh, wait. That's just Randal Farbloss.

You're right. What was I thinking?

You are such a freak.

At least I'm not a freak who thinks he sees dead people.

haha   haha

haha

haha

heh

I'm dipping my feet in

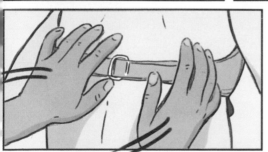

GASP

SPLASHHHHH

Come on! Get in!

Yeah, Marjie May. Don't be such a boy!

Knock knock

HAUNTED

Hey, bug. Can I come in?

nod

I might have caught a ghost today.

Is that right?

I was down by the lake, right past The Scoop.

Tonya still hadn't put up the new flavor.

I could tell something was off.

Turns out, a hotdog man burned to death in that *exact* spot over twenty years ago because of a bad wire in his food truck.

One wire.

There are a lot of wires in this house, Dad.

And tons of—don't touch that.

Tons of people have died on that beach.

The articles are there, see?

I do see. It looks like the *Finster Bay Gazette* moved its offices into your bedroom.

And Dad,

there was a girl there talking to herself.

Isn't that weird?!

Well, honey, let's not be too hasty to judge.

I bet she was talking to a ghost.

Mmhm. Hey, Liza?

I mean, there was no one else there.

Eliza. Sweetie.

I'd love to hear more about this later, but I have to take Gracie to gymnastics,

and your mom is at Kenzie's soccer game.

Are you going to be okay here by yourself?

I'm not going to be here by myself.

inhale

I'm going to the darkroom.

exhale

And you're sure Miss Linse is okay with that?

It's August 23rd.

Right.

She gave me permission to use it over the summer.

The last day of summer is August 24th.

This is the 23rd.

Okay, bug, be back in time for dinner.

Yep.

39

Ghosts exist. I'm going to prove it,

me and Lorraine here.

The darkroom is where I'll make that happen.

Photography is all about what you see, but you have to develop it in a room where you can barely see anything.

I don't mind the dark, though, or what's in the dark. I didn't even mind it when I was five.

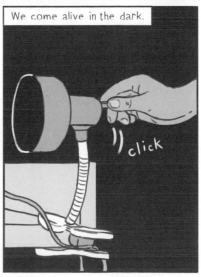

Jimmy Prickle said it's because I blend in so well with the dark.

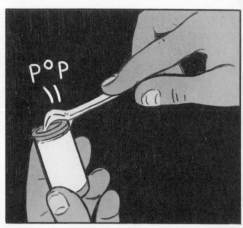

POP

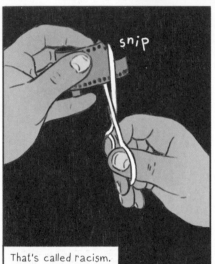

snip

That's called racism.

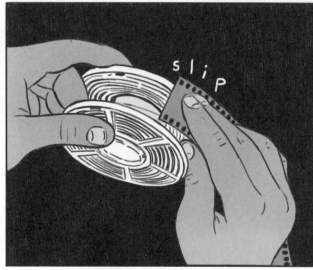

slip

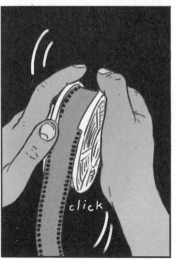

click

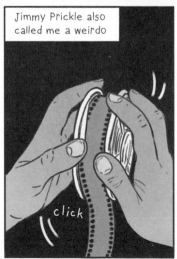

Jimmy Prickle also called me a weirdo

click

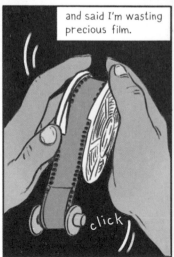

and said I'm wasting precious film.

click

I wanted to tell him that he is a waste of precious space on Earth, but I didn't.

click

That's called making good choices.

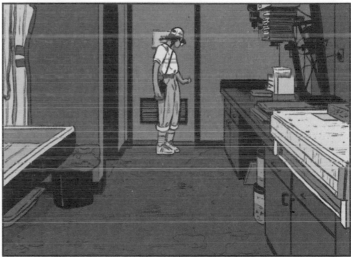

I do that sometimes.

6:37 AM

6:38 AM

7:51 AM

7:58 AM

9:30 AM

10:42 AM

11:21 AM

11:33 AM

11:34 AM

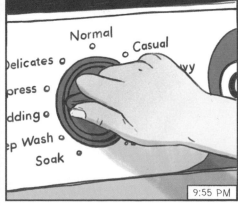

It sure is awful quiet in here.

Yeah, that's what happens when washing machines work properly.

Maybe you could do something to make it, you know,

less quiet.

You want me to break the machines for old time's sake?

No. You could play piano for us.

Like that time back at the old house, when you—

Wendell, I can't. I need to finish this.

Tessi has this whole "coordinated first day outfit" decree, and knowing her, it's been signed by the mayor.

And it's almost eleven.

I don't like eighth grade.

Well, luckily you'll never have to go.

I'm sorry, I didn't mean that.

Look, another time, okay?

I don't want to be tired on the first day.

Okay.

Night.

Collapse!
Collapse!

Marj, it's nearly two.

What are you still doing up?

And what's with all these sheets?

Sorry, Dad. I'll clean them up.

And then, good gravy, get some sleep.

Yep. I will.

yawwwn

went out for a run. Have a great first day of school! love, Dad

boop beep bo doop

Owen, it's almost 7:30.

You need to get ready.

beep beep tchhhhh WEEEEE

Owen!

Come eat, and get ready to go.

I'm taking that game away if you're not over here in ten seconds.

mmmmgh

SLUMP

Are you ready for first grade?

I think I have ammonia.

You don't.

It's too nice out to go to school.

It was too nice to stay inside and play video games all summer, but you managed to do that.

You're also not sick.

Owen, eat.

We're leaving in fifteen minutes whether you're ready or not.

And first graders don't forget the kid who shows up in pajamas on the first day.

Morning.

Good morning.

You okay?

Fine.

Tessi Renae.

Attitude.

I think you can handle one day a week after school.

What do you have to do?

Nothing.

It's just a mother-daughter—

Mom! God! Can you please stop talking?!

Marjorie, do you talk to your father like this?

I know Sasha and her mom get along just fine.

And *they* socialize.

Sasha and Rajani. Sasha and Rajani. They baked...whatever it was...

that Indian dough thing for the dance team fundraiser last year, and we never heard the end of it.

Oh, so this is a jealousy thing.

No, Tessi, this is a parent thing.

No! Explode!

He's talking about his game.

Not...not you.

You can spare your Wednesdays for an hour with your mother.

Okay, God! Whatever!

Okay, fine.

Fine!

Thanks for the ride.

Mmhm.

...trying out for soccer?

Dance, remember? ...eleven hours a week.

...already signed up.

...thought you'd join, Tessi... athletic...

You make the rest of us look bad, Colton!

Oh, *stop.*

So, what is our Marjie May going to join?

Oh, uh, sports are not my thing.

Ha! Don't I know it!

Little Miss Beethoven over here.

Actually, I don't really play much anymore.

We'll find you **something** you can be good at.

What about photography?

There's no club or anything.

But I'm in the darkroom almost every day after school.

Usually alone...

but sometimes Miss Linse is there.

These are some photos I developed yesterday.

From when I saw you, remember?

Talking to yourself by the lake?

Some couples are like those buy-one-get-one deals on cheap shampoo that nobody wanted even one of.

Oh... they're not a couple.

He and I—

I mean— we're all friends.

Your photos are, um,

nice.

I could teach you, you know. Photography.

It's not really my thing.

So, what *is* your thing?

Huh?

What *is* your thing?

shrug

And I wasn't hearing things!

Your topic is...

ghost photography?

Yep.

And you've taken this course before?

Eliza took DP II last year,

so she's joining us as an independent study student.

So, you already know about blurs from long shutter speeds and dust on the negatives and all that?

Yes, I've been doing this for years.

So, you know the likelihood of those white spots being "ghosts" is...

let's say, zero percent?

Okay, how about we look at these photos from an artistic and compositional perspective?

Would anyone like to comment?

Well, I think they're lovely, Eliza.

I look forward to seeing more work from you this semester.

Okay, everyone.

Let's look at the syllabus.

...and if you recall, last year we covered light...

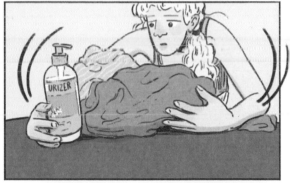

Marjorie?

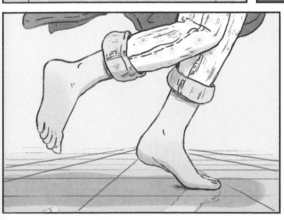

Don't worry about the laundry. I can do it.

There were some with stains.

Oh—

So, you went to the quilt thing?

Oh, no, this is an old one.

I'm just... reorganizing.

Isn't the point to go to the meetings?

And, like, finish the quilts for charity?

It's just a group of your mom's friends.

It's casual.

And I'm starting a new one.

Your mom was so good, it's hard to keep up.

Her friends just show up whenever they can, you know?

You know I'd take care of it if you'd show me your "secret" technique.

I keep asking.

No, Dad, it's fine. I told you. It's, like, a complicated twenty-step process.

It's easier if I do it.

Okay... well,

leave the rest up to me, at least.

It's good when I can keep busy.

You did your share last year, helping in the laundromat after your mom...

You have a life now.

So, you know, live it.

slide

Am I the only kid who wishes we got homework on the first day?

School. Laundry. Homework. Bed. Repeat. That's what I know.

Before Mom died, we had our things that we did together.

Like playing piano. Looking for beach glass. Eating popcorn and Milk Duds for dinner at the theater when an old movie was showing.

And now what? My thing is just...laundry.

slump

tick tick
tick tick
tick tick

tick tick
tick tick
tick tick

knock
knock
knock

Hey, Wendell.

You busy tonight?

Okay.

I can't believe we're out! At the movies!

And no one will see me?

No one ever comes here.

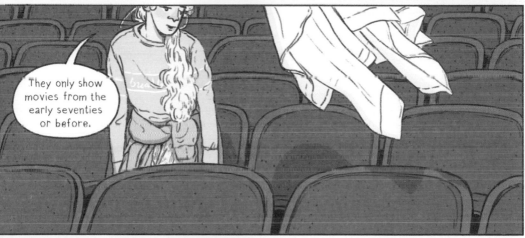

They only show movies from the early seventies or before.

Sometimes they'll show an eighties classic like *Ferris Bueller* or *The Goonies*, though,

and people go to those.

Who's Ferris Gooler?

You have much to learn.

Marjorie?

Eliza! H-hi!

I thought I'd have the theater to myself. But it's okay if you're here.

Are you a frequenter of The Rubin?

Uh...n-no.

N-not really.

I'm here all the time.

I love old black and white movies.

This one's in color, though.

This kind of reminds me of the darkroom, you know? It's old and mechanical,

and there's a sort of quiet that's... warm and snug, even when people are dying on screen.

Plus, I usually have the theater to myself.

Uh, yeah...

Well— Who's your friend?

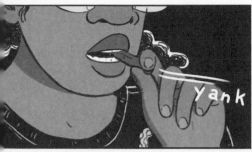

He's behind that curtain.

They should not be going in there.

puh

the new paranormal

I told them.

RUBIN

THE GHOST WEARS PRADA
WHAT A GIRL HAUNTS

The G

It doesn't make sense that ghosts are always the villains.

Some of them were good humans, probably.

I mean, I expect I'll be bitter when I die. Don't you?

Not a monster, though.

Not a monster.

Nope.

RUBIN

We better get home.

Okay, bye.

Wait!

And now Dad thinks he's involved in some solo game of musical chairs and can't sit down unless,

oh, I don't know, the earth stops turning.

He says he doesn't need my help, even though he can't finish *anything*.

And I was the laundry girl.

That was my thing.

Normal teenagers are supposed to have hobbies and interests and bucket lists of things to do befo—

Before they die?

sift

I wanted to go to a ball.

Wait, what?

Before I died, I wanted to go to a fancy ball.

You know,

with the puffy gowns and drippy lights and flowers. And the buccaneer.

heh

Boutonniere.

You like to dance?

I was going to dance in the ballet, too. Maybe as the Nutcracker Prince.

hahaha!

hahaha

What's so funny?

hehe

Boys can't dance ballet?

No, of course they can.

I just can't picture *you* being a dancer.

It's too late now, anyway.

September 17

September 21

WENDELL AND MR. CHICKEN

A PUPPET SHOW

September 24

OBITUARIES

September 29

October 1

October 2

For...?

I found a club for you to join.

You. Are. Welcome.

Well, for me to join.

And *then* I thought it would be super great for us to do together.

Right?

So, what is it?

Student council.

As in the group that makes decisions and plans events and has to lead the people?

That doesn't really sound like me.

Oh, come *on*, Marjie May.

Please? Please, please, please? I don't want to do this stupid thing alone!

Stupid?

Well, some of it is stupid.

Are you joining?

Can't. Soccer.

But we get to plan the fall dance.

I already have a *bunch* of ideas.

Palace Dreams, Up in the Clouds, A Night at the Circus, Stars and Stripes—

you know, like retro patriotism—

Enchanted Forest, Enchanted *Bayou*—

Stone age!

Okay, fine. Go on.

Are those themes for the fall dance?

Um, yeah.

It should be something original.

Maybe something with ghosts, since it's only a couple weeks after Halloween.

This concerns people who are actually going to the dance.

Maybe I am.

Whatever.

Meet me in room 114 in five minutes for the first meeting.

Wait, it's right now?

My mom's giving you a ride, remember? You can't leave without me!

So...

Are you going to photograph the dance?

Why would I do that?

I mean, you're always taking pictures.

Can't I go just to go?

I just didn't think you would.

Developing film is a delicate process.

When you remove it from the camera, it can't be exposed to any light whatsoever.

You have to agitate the film in a canister—

600 milliliters of film developer fluid, 600 of room temperature water (room temperature is important)—

and do it just right, so the film is evenly submerged.

tick
tick
tick

Then there's the stop bath,

fixer,

fixer remover,

and photo-safe soap,

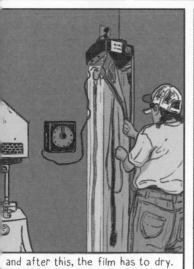

and after this, the film has to dry.

You can't make any mistakes. The teensiest mistake will ruin the whole process. All your photos: gone forever.

Humans are delicate, too.

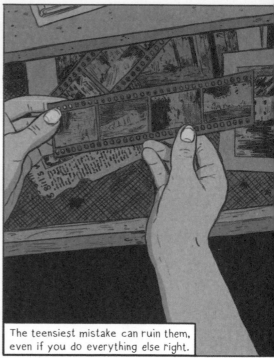

The teensiest mistake can ruin them, even if you do everything else right.

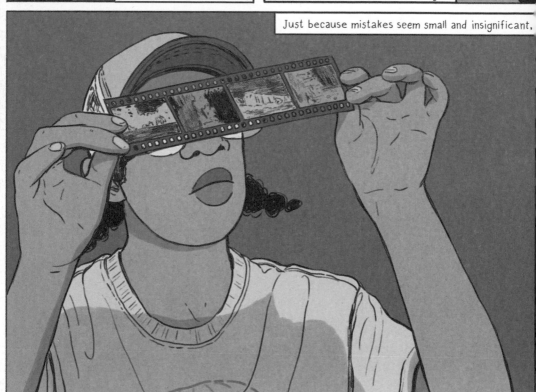

Just because mistakes seem small and insignificant,

doesn't mean they are.

Marjorie Glatt in the house!

Marjorie! I didn't know you were joining.

I invited her.

Nice.

Yeah, as if you need an invitation from Tessi to join student council.

All right, knuckleheads.

Your king is speaking.

Now, as faculty advisor for this fine council of misfits, I would normally go around asking what you think we should do as a committee this year.

Then, I would scribble your ideas, probably a lot of terrible ones, on the board with this here baby blue chalk.

Which, of course, I would later erase from the board, but not from my mind—God help me—and just use the curriculum the administration is forcing me to use.

Now, who votes we skip all that and pass out these totalitarian handouts instead?

Great! The people voted! Democracy!

So, there are the usuals, like fundraisers and dances and such.

Student
~~~~ 15-

But we also need to work on improving our culture.

For example, social issues, anti-bullying, developing ways to be more...

Are you free after school on Thursday?

Why?

We're going dress shopping.

For the dance?

It's a month away.

I don't even know if I'm going.

What are you talking about?

I don't have... no one's asked me.

I don't have a date yet, either.

...doing the best I can!

...I'm not...can't be in three places at once...

I thought you were canceling...

Why is that my fault?!

And what about Eliza? ...splitting our time between her sisters?

Eliza is fine! Her photography...alone, anyway.

Knock knock.

Hey, bug? How's it going?

Fine.

Good, good. So, listen.

I know your mom and I have been spending a lot of time with your sisters, lately.

Those little monsters are time hogs.

It's fine. Lorraine and I are busy.

And that's great.

But maybe you could think about joining some activities with other kids.

Why didn't you give student council a try?

I swear I said less than forty embarrassing things.

I was busy developing.

Uhh...

Prints, Dad. Developing prints.

I just think you should branch out a little.

Make some friends.

What about Marjorie? You should ask her to do something.

Can you do that for me?

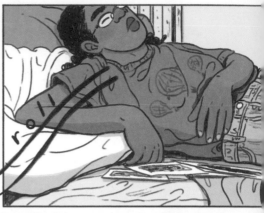

Okay.

There you go!

Most of my work is at school.

I need to protect it from Tweedle Klutz and Tweedle Syrup Fingers.

Not a lot of people up here.

No. I need to focus on ghosts for my paranormal portfolio.

You might photograph those showy neighbors of ours. Everyone can see right through them.

Why don't you try some portraits?

Or the soccer game? Change it up a bit?

Just think about it, okay?

Mom took a lot of pictures. She said photos can reveal secrets about our own stories. She hated knowing how much we miss—how little we actually see in the world.

We were on a picnic the morning before she died. I don't even remember if it was sunny or what we ate or what she was wearing.

She had brought her camera, but I don't know what ever happened to the pictures.

:reeeeak

I don't know what all I missed.

What are you doing down here?

You can join me.

I should really clean this mess up.

Oh.

Can I take some with me?

Yeah, yeah. Take them upstairs.

There's another project that will never be finished.

beep beep boop

CRASH

beep beep

CH-CHING

beep boing beep beep boop WEEE

Owen.

Hey, Owen!

Hm

You should come look through these pictures with me.

I have to stop the trolls!

Marjorie.

Psst, Marjorie.

Wendell! What are you doing?!

Why weren't you in the laundromat tonight?

Are you not my friend anymore?

That's ridiculous. Of course I am.

You need to get back down there before someone wakes up and sees you!

Can we go to the movies with Eliza again?

I like her.

creeeeeak

Wendell, go downstairs!

But—

I *promise* we will do something together this weekend, okay?

Saturday night. You and me.

Now go!

Here's how it goes: You swim 20 yards out,

locate this brick at the bottom,

retrieve it,

and swim it back.

You have a minute and forty seconds. So, who's up?

All right, then, boys. You're up, Grover.

Huh?

Time's up!

Tut tut. Not a single hero.

Okay, ladies, bring the humiliation.

SPLASHHHHHHH

fidget

He's her *dad.*

I bet she was way over time.

As if she cares about *boys'* attention, anyway.

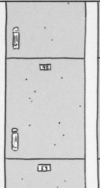

Do you want to go to Spinney's with me this Saturday night?

It's a pumpkin farm that—

I know Spinney's.

Um...

I actually already have plans this weekend.

Work stuff. My dad is making me help him in the laundromat.

Oh. Okay.

Sorry. See you later.

RINNNNGGGGGGGG

Marjorie!

Over here!

Shopping time!

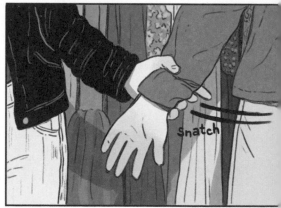

What is Colton doing here?

I invited him, dummy.

Isn't that a bit presumptuous?

I mean, he doesn't even have a date...

does he?

So? He can't be thinking about it?

I was just...

I was kind of hoping he would...

Ask you? Has he said something?

No.

Well—I mean...

who knows if he even wants to go to the stupid dance, anyway.

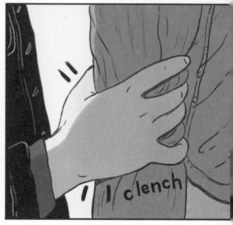

And I bet I could pick out a few boys from the soccer team who will *never* find dates.

So, why don't we all go together? As a group?

That's what *single* people do, right?

Uh, yeah...I don't really do dances.

You girls make them a way bigger deal than they are.

But every girl wants you as *her* date, Colton.

Yeah, call a girl your date and suddenly she thinks she's in a committed relationship with you.

Dude, what the heck? I'm not going if you're not!

I'll buy your dinner.

All right, now we're getting somewhere. Make it three dinners.

Even better.

Okay, so Marjie and Sash and I will find matching dresses, and you boys can match us all, okay?

Whatever.

See?

Problem solved.

What are you doing on Saturday night, again?

I told you: I already have plans. I can't get out of them.

Oh, that's too bad.

Looks like it's just going to be you and me, Colton.

What?

I thought we could go to Spinney's as a group.

But you already have solid, irreversible plans, so—

No, it's fine!

I'll be there. It won't be a problem.

Oh. That's wonderful.

inhale

slide

Guess what tomorrow is?!

Listen, Wendell...

It's SATURDAY.

So what are we doing?! Movie? Hide and seek? Let's have a staring contest.

There's been a change of plans. I can't hang out tomorrow.

But you promised.

I know, I'm sorry.

Tessi's making me go to Spinney's with her.

I don't have a choice. I tried to get out of it.

You promised.

Sunday, okay? We'll do something Sunday.

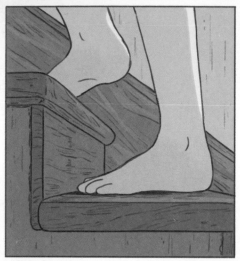

This way!

Colton, you're such a trailblazer!

What can I say? I'm husky! Ha!

Okay, we've totally passed that cornstalk, already.

We're going to die in here!

Marjie May, do you have any water?

Do you mean now, or should I ration it for our survival?

Now. Do you have it?

What time is it?

Uh, a little after six. Why?

shove

I just remembered. I have to go.

What are you talking about?

I have to get out of this maze.

Come on, girls!

I think this is going to be our family Christmas card.

People say my family is weird, but for my parents and sisters, they mean it in a good way.

I think I'm the wrong kind of weird, which I didn't know you could be.

Some people don't like feeling invisible,

but I feel way too visible.

If I were a ghost, I could choose how and when to be seen,

and that sounds like a much better deal.

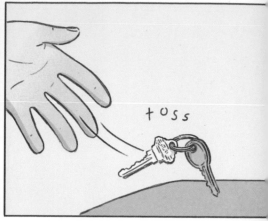

toss

Why would you do that?!

yawwWWh

Why aren't we at Spinney's?

You *snuck* into my bag?

Did you think I'd pull a sheet out in public and casually let it follow me around all night?

I'm not just a sheet!

And you promised! You promised we'd hang out!

It's not easy being trapped in here every night.

A washing machine starts to lose its thrill after hundreds of spin cycles.

Look, people don't believe in ghosts. They don't *want* to believe in ghosts.

If they saw you, they'd go nuts.

I'm trying to protect you.

Protect us, or yourself?

What?

You don't want them knowing you're friends with a bunch of ghosts.

That's not true!

We have to be smart about this!

No, *you* should be smart.

And who knows what they'd try to do to you!

Has no one seen *Ghostbusters*?

You don't know what would happen.

Neither do you. We can't risk it.

159

There's this thing called a latent image.

It's the image on the film or print that has been exposed to light, but not developed yet.

It's there, but you can't see it. Like a ghost image.

There's a sort of magic to making it appear. Not like "ala kazam" magic. It's like...

the darkness is hiding.

nudge

All it takes is light and chemicals
and patience to make it appear.

Humans have hidden darkness, too, like secrets and sadness.
But you can't just stick a person in developer fluid, can you?

PLOP

What's this?

A loupe.

What is it?

It's a magnifier.

So you can look at your negatives up close before you develop your contact sheet.

To test your exposures.

I'm going to the light table now.

Hey, wait!

I wanted to invite you to go trick-or-treating with us on Thursday.

With Tessi?

Tessi will be there, but it's going to be a group of us.

It'll be fun.

Thursday?

Six-o-clock at my house.

You're not going as an antisocial loser, are you?

I'm not going.

A little too old for this stuff now?

First grade rebellion?

You're not getting any of my candy.

Earth to Owen.

Why aren't you going?

I don't wanna.

Owen, it's trick-or-treat, and you don't want to go?

Seriously?

YANK

HEY!

NO!

Look at me—

Give it back!

Tell me why you're not going.

Tell me, and I'll give it back.

NO!

sob

Is this because of Mom? Because she used to take us?

She a-always—made—my costume.

Didn't you already rake this morning?

Well, you know, the leaves keep falling.

Dad, Owen's not trick-or-treating.

And you're just going to let him stay home?

Yeah, I know.

If he doesn't want to go...

Of course he wants to go!

He misses Mom.

You need to take him. And, I don't know, help him with a costume in the next...

hour.

I...

I have a lot to do around here.

You can't keep pushing everything away.

Mom's gone, and Owen needs you!

Why don't you stop worrying about the five leaves that fell since this morning, and worry about him?

I'm doing the best I can!

I got him a whole bag of candy.

He's set for weeks.

Way to give a two percent effort, Dad.

Are we going, or what?

We're waiting on one more.

Uhh, what is *she* doing here?

My dad made me invite her.

Just pretend she's not here.

This'll be fun.

Wendell! Hi!

I'm not sick.

I'm not allowed out with Marjorie's friends.

Neither am I.

DEAD END

You were out with them tonight, though.

Not really.

rustle

People think an invitation is enough, even if they act like they don't want you there.

At least you were invited.

crinkle

It doesn't feel like it.

You seem sad.

Sorry.

Do you want to talk about it?

I don't think anyone cares, except maybe my parents,

but they probably feel like it's something they should do.

Do you ever feel like that?

THE GOOD GR LES

That is my exact situation.

Sometimes I feel like a ghost, but maybe a ghost in the wrong place, you know?

My dad says to "be myself." But see, he's wrong, because that's what I'm doing, and it doesn't work.

I think he has friends, though.

Sorry...

Sometimes I can make people uncomfortable.

Uh, yeah, I wear this to protect against evil spirits.

You need one to protect against evil humans.

I don't think it's ever going to get better.

Hey, I want to show you something!

This is as far as I can go.

Why?

Because I'm scared, too, of the water.

And I'm scared *I'm* not going to get better.

That's ridiculous.

I had a bad experience with a lake.

But you're still alive, right?

Well...

You're going to have to swim eventually.

I mean, if you want to pass gym class.

I was the only one to pass the brick challenge, though. It was cool.

My dad thinks that's how I'll make friends.

By swimming?

By being really good at swimming, I guess.

Will you be my friend if I swim?

Where have you been?

With Eliza.

What were you thinking? I told you to stay here, didn't I?

I can't believe you snuck out. *Again.*

Do you know how many people saw you?

What if something would have happened, and they found out—

Nothing happened!

The whole point of trick-or-treating is to get candy.

You can't even *eat* candy.

Stop trying to fit in, because you can't.

You can't fit in.

What happened with Eliza?

She says she feels like a ghost, which I can confirm is *not* a great feeling.

Wendell?

I don't get scared. Ghost photographers can't.

They spend all their time in places with a lot of ghost stories.

Like this one.

Wendell?

creeeak

rustle

SLAM

AHHHHH!

You dare enter our resting place?

slide

Maybe you should join us.

Join us! Join us!

What is this?

sob

Trying to keep us away?

Snatch

Bad mistake.

VENKMAN

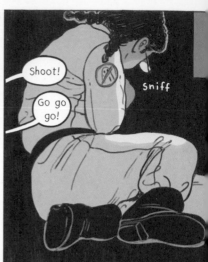

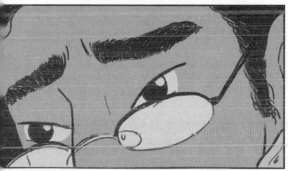

Get out here!

You're never going to guess what happened last night.

I'm never going to try.

We all dressed up in sheets and trapped the freak in that old lighthouse down by The Brine and Dine.

I never thought it would actually work! The dweeb totally spazzed.

You're kidding, right?

It was pretty funny.

And I stole that dumb evil protection or whatever pin.

It's sitting like a trophy in my bedroom.

Why would you do that?

Um, because it was hilarious?

And you think so, too?

I mean... it was Tessi's idea.

You have to admit that Eliza makes it so easy.

To be jerks? That's on you, not on her.

She hunts *ghosts.*

So?

So, it's pathetic! Do *you* believe in ghosts?

I...

no—

The whole thing is stupid, right?

This whole thing *is* stupid.

Exactly.

Whoa, ladies, calm down.

We should go grab some cider at Colleen's.

I have to get home.

For what?

Nothing.

I'm busy, okay?

Me too.

...stole...evil protection...pin.

Hey! I'm not stupid!

You can't trick—huh?

Because we have to try what the therapist says!

I'm so done with these stupid sessions!

201

...fifteen minutes...

...yoga pants and get your mat...

slide

202

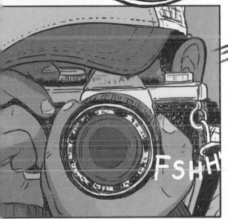

Where did you go this time?

Nowhere.

Really.

I'm not anywhere, am I?!

Ghosts don't exist!

Ghosts are *stupid!*

Why do you care?

What are you holding?

Nothing.

Is that Eliza's pin?

How—

I'm trying to help her!

I told you to stay out of this!

Did you know there are some ghosts in the Land of Ghosts who *chose* to be there?

Because they were too sad in the Land of Humans?

And they *all* wish it would have been different.

That they had a second chance—

If you're talking about Eliza right now, you're wrong.

She hardly ever acts sad, and she's never said she wants to be a ghost.

She just wants to photograph one.

I've spent more time with her than you have.

YANK

And I'm not even allowed out of this house!

Whoa there, Eliza.

Slow down. This isn't I-90.

I have to get to the darkroom *now.*

I got one.

A *ghost.*

I came in yesterday. I couldn't tell, but the film should be dry, and I can enlarge them, and...Miss Linse!

I got one! I *know* it!

Eliza, homeroom starts in ten minutes!

Leslie, did you see this yet?! Is that Tessi and her *mom?*

Walter, come look at this!

Was this you?

Oh, um. I was photographing the ghost. See?

rrrriPPPP

Bad mistake.

Eliza!

Eliza, you okay?

Where's all your stuff?

I think I'm done.

Done?

Done with what?

Is this what it's like for ghosts?

You don't have a name or face, and you're not really anybody in particular?

You can't be judged by what they see or remember.

I know I'm Eliza, but nobody else has to.

He doesn't know it.

They don't.
Nobody knows it.

Ghosts are better off.

What the—

Eliza?

What are you doing home so early?

Did something happen?

They stole my work.

Who?

Oh, hon. That's awful.

They're probably jealous, you know?

They hate me.

No one hates you.

You just have to reach out a little and make some friends.

You can't sit around waiting for them to come to you.

...did you...?

...Eliza?

So, what is this Sam Heem, Sallo-ween thing again?

It's pronounced "Sah-win."

I don't know.

All I could get out of her was that it's not Halloween.

And that "we need to welcome the spirits as they cross the boundary into our world."

How fun. Is there cake?

No kids are going to come to this.

Why did we let her do this?

You try telling her "no."

What's this?

It's cider for the dead.

slump

225

Hey, bug. So, what's on the agenda for tonight?

We start with the Samhain feast, but we have to offer food to the spirits, first,

through him.

Then we light the candles and have our bonfire ceremony,

where we move around it clockwise.

I don't think anyone's coming.

You know, kids are probably busy for Halloween.

It's November first.

And a Friday night.

But your Granddaddy Cal is here, right?

Calvin?

Now, I'm going to be honest with you, girlie.

I didn't know what this whole Samhain thing was,

so I brought a gift just in case.

Here, Dad.

And don't you be offering it to them dead folk.

Know what that is?

A Pentax K1000.

Boy, did I capture some good memories on that bad boy.

You know something, Liza Bean?

You don't need them other kids steering your lifeboat.

I want you to take that there camera and see the world, the way you want to see it.

Eliza?

229

This whole "ghost" thing...

maybe you should take a break for a while.

Don't give them a reason to make things hard for you.

nod

Good.

And leaving school early—what were you thinking?

Never again, you hear?

I'm taking a box to donate to the shelter. Anything you want to get rid of?

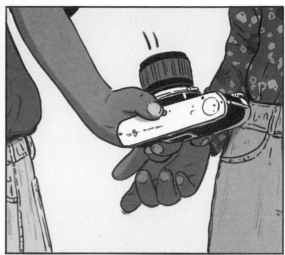

slide

I didn't get to go trick-or-treating!

Are you kidding?!

I did everything but drag you out the door to get you to go!

SOB

Hey, hey.

I know. I shouldn't have been so hard on you.

I miss Mom, too. But you have me, okay?

And we can still do everything we used to, just the two of us.

But no sweets, right? I know how much you hate those.

What? No!

I'm kidding.

Why don't we trick-or-treat right now?

Huh?

Of course
it is.

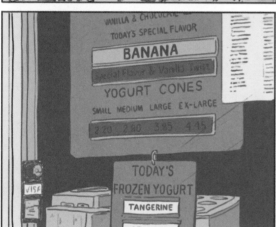

Hey!

What's with the costumes?

What's with the solitude?

Huh?

Nothing. Tessi's usually with you, that's all.

She's been kind of messed up after what Eliza did to her.

What *Eliza* did?

Well, you saw the photo, didn't you? The whole school did.

I'm sure Tessi will get her revenge, somehow.

Ha, check.

She ripped up Eliza's work and dumped it into the lake behind the old lighthouse.

Hey, she deserves it.

Taking photos outside someone's house late at night, like some kind of predator?

That's creepy, dude.

Come on, Owen, we have to go.

What the heck, Marjorie? What is with you?

It's pretty clear who's seeing things that aren't there, and it's not Eliza.

What are you talking about?

You act like you're this great person, and then you pull something like this?

Tessi did this! I never did anything to Eliza!

You were at the lighthouse, weren't you?

You let it happen.

Wendell! What are you doing?!

I'm running away! Flying the coop! Blowing this popsicle stand!

Who is that?

Go ahead and lie, you liar!

mmmgh

He's a *ghost*. Okay?!

He lives here! With, like, thirty other ghosts, and they bring their crazy ghost shampoo.

And yes, I lied and hid it for the past year, and I'm sorry, but—

there it is!

Yeah. Okay.

I don't think he heard you.

I'm sorry. I'm sorry for saying you don't fit in here.

And I'm sorry for Tessi and Colton and for hanging you out to dry.

I mean, like, not on laundry day.

I promise you, I will NEVER let anyone come between our friendship again.

Okay.

I'll untie Baby Timmy.

Does that mean I can talk now?

No.

Good, because I need your help with something.

So, they're torn-up photos? And you know they're here?

Or so I've been told.

There! Look!

I bet a ton of them sunk...

You leave that up to me!

Wendell!

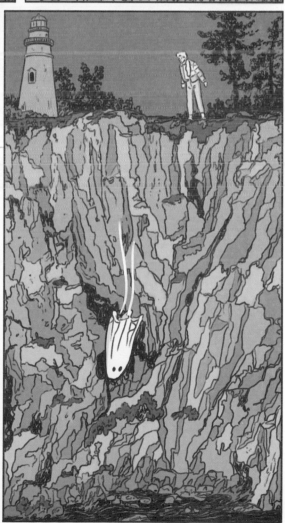

SPLASH

Wendell! How...

You were underwater!

Eliza helped.

Look, there's writing on the back of some of them.

Is it still a life when you're a ghost?

Ask me to the ghost dance

Marjorie?

You have to do something.

Look at those shining faces.

Don't you love meetings before school?

We're a week away from the fall dance,

so we need to make sure we're all ready for a loud, sweaty, terrible night.

fidget

Kayla, have the caterers—wow!

Marjorie wants to speak?

Stand down, everyone.

Go ahead.

I'd like to propose a change...

to the dance.

I know it's short notice.

Is she serious?

What?

It's hard...coming to a place every day where people judge you and ignore you and...

hurt you.

And dances make all of that worse.

You get judged not only for who you are,

but also your dress and your hair and what random person you got to be your date.

What about the students who already bought their dresses?

You can still wear them for pictures and dinner.

It'll be like a full-body masquerade.

I guess a masquerade could be cool.

It's never been done before. Like, newsworthy!

Put it to a vote?

Who's in?

All right.

Let's get planning.

...I mean, what **was** that?

Do you realize you just ruined the entire dance for me?

Not everything is about you, okay?

Maybe you shouldn't come in our group.

Not with me **or** Colton.

I accept your un-invitation.

You can still go—

I **am** still going.

With who?

I guess you'll never know.

Have you seen Fliza?

I don't think she's here today.

knock
knock

Hey, Mr. Duncan?

That's my name.

Do you know where Eliza was today?

Is the father supposed to know that? Oh, man.

She was in school, wasn't she?

Oh...

Yeah, sorry.

I-I meant where she is now?

Did you check the darkroom?

Oh, yeah. That's, um...

Good idea.

Marjorie!

I finished putting together Eliza's pictures, and—

That's great, Wendell,

but I've spent the entire evening looking for Eliza and can't find her anywhere.

I just had the entire dance redesigned for her,

tug

but it's fine!

Read the notes on the back!

It's like she's saying goodbye. We have to do something!

We can find her if it's not too late.

mmgh

Marjorie!

The old lighthouse!

pant
pant
pant

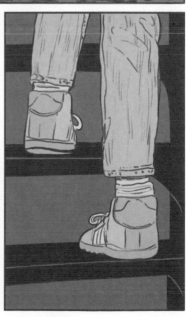

I know my friends can be bullies.

I didn't realize it bothered you that much.

It's not just your friends.

But...I never did anything.

I mean, I didn't—I never joined in.

You let it happen.

That's still bullying.

272

But I would have never known how you were feeling unless you told me all of this.

And I was feeling pretty bad about my life last year. After I lost my mom, things got really messed up.

But you can't give up.

You'd miss out on so much.

You don't know that.

Yeah, I do. I know what it's like to be fragile.

But sometimes people need to know something's fragile in order to handle it right.

Like how they stamp mailed packages.

Except, there's nothing more delicate than a life.

Now I know. I can try to help.

And I know some others who can, too.

Guys, come in here.

Are they...

Mmhm.

For a freak who sees dead people, I've been pretty blind to what's in front of me.

Last year, I was the one who felt like a ghost.

How did I end up on the other side?

You never know what's going on inside someone else's head—how they're hurting—

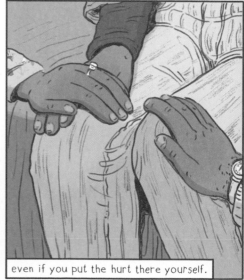

even if you put the hurt there yourself.

Maybe we need to stop thinking only about what we see,

and focus on learning what is actually there.

Are you coming with me to deliver the paperwork, or what?

I see you have a new bestie.

Looks like helping you become popular was a total waste.

yawwwn

She was having suicidal thoughts, Tessi.

Scoff

I hope you're happy.

Please.

It's not my fault she's so sensitive.

So it's okay to be mean to sensitive people?

You have NO idea—

How do you even know?

I found her, Tessi.

She was, like, alone in a lighthouse, and...

it was bad.

Alone in a lighthouse.

You didn't see her.

If I would have gotten there later, who knows what could have happened.

But I didn't know what to do.

At least now her parents know, and—

Her *dad* knows?!

Mr. Duncan?

wipe

I'm just dropping off the ticket sale paperwork.

You might have saved her life, you know?

I'm afraid I could have...not been able to.

My friend, Wendell...

I should have listened.

But Eliza— she's the one who asked for help.

swivel

Some people are lifeguards. Others need to be saved.

She said this to me.

Is she okay?

She starts therapy next week.

That's good.

rub

Would it be okay if Eliza comes to the dance with me and my friends?

Oh... well...

I'm not sure it's the best thing...for her to be socializing with, uh,

some of the other eighth graders.

I'm not talking about Tessi.

I guess that would be all right.

Mr. Duncan?

Everyone has ghosts.

I think we all need to learn that there's no shame in letting them out.

This is SO COOL, Marjorie.

You said you wanted a ghost dance.

And so did you, Wendell.

It's just like I pictured!

May I have this dance?

Are you having fun?

A ghost dance was a bad idea.

What?

It's just...

what happens when I have to take off the sheet?

When I can't hide who I am?

Will you dance with me, Wendell?

Really?

You'll always be my best friend, you know that?

Even when you're ninety-two?

At least until I'm ninety-one.

I wish I was alive to be ninety-one with you.

I'm sorry you can't have the life you wanted.

But you save lives, Wendell.

You saved mine.

Maybe saving lives can be my thing!

Yeah.

I think it's both of ours.

297

Knock knock.

Eliza, baby...

I couldn't let you get rid of this.

It's you.

How is it that we're all people, we all feel the same basic emotions,

but somehow we still can't understand each other?

What a trip.

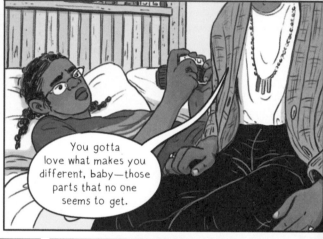

You gotta love what makes you different, baby—those parts that no one seems to get.

Like ghost photography.

Right.

302

And how people like Jimmy Prickle call me a weirdo.

Would you rather be a weirdo, or Jimmy Prickle?

Weirdo.

Exactly.

And Eliza?

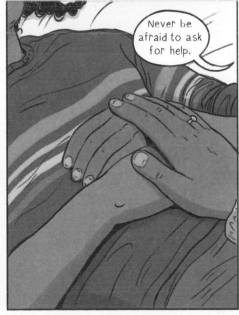

Never be afraid to ask for help.

303

This is every photo box I could find.

The basement is a mess again.

I did finish my first quilt, though.

Yeah, I saw. It looks... quilt-like.

But I'm glad you finished.

Would you look at that.

Could I have this?

Sure. It's yours.

I mean, you scare me. And ghosts don't even scare me.

But you didn't deserve to be hurt.

I'm going to go now.

Hey!

No one deserves to be hurt.

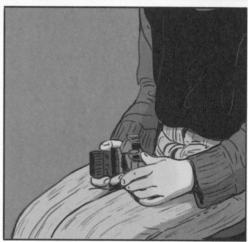

You have
a camera.

It was my
mom's.

Could you teach me how to use it?

There's still a roll of film in here.

What?

Yeah.

There were photos...from the last day with my mom.

Maybe...

I can develop it for you if you want.

Can we do it together?

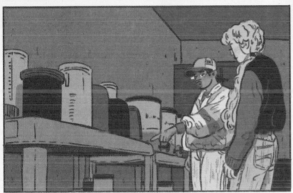

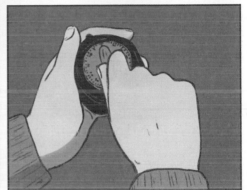

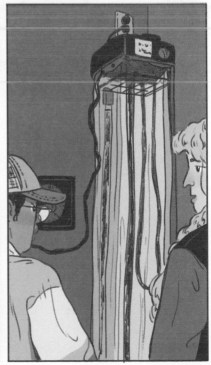

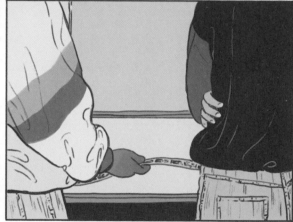

ACKNOWLEDGMENTS

My editor, Grace Scheipeter, for her attentiveness, patience, and friendship, especially in handling ghosts and delicate situations.

My other editor, Andrea Colvin, who laid the groundwork for a lifelong adventure, and who inspires me every day.

The entire Oni Press team for their diligence and endless support.

Hannah Mann, the most wonderful agent, who has helped me keep my sanity.

My friends from Lion Forge and Andrews McMeel, who continue to boost my confidence.

Heather Brand and her darkroom photography class for their crucial insight and demonstrations.

Jasmine Walls for her discernment in reviewing the story's sensitive subject matter.

My friends, family, and cat for their constant love and encouragement.

If you or someone you know is struggling with thoughts of suicide, contact the National Suicide Prevention Lifeline at 1-800-273-8255 or SuicidePreventionLifeline.org.

Designed by Sarah Rockwell
Edited by Andrea Colvin
Additional Editing by Grace Scheipeter
Consulting reader: Jasmine Walls

PUBLISHED BY ONI-LION FORGE PUBLISHING GROUP, LLC.

James Lucas Jones, president & publisher • Sarah Gaydos, editor in chief • Charlie Chu, e.v.p.
of creative & business development • Brad Rooks, director of operations • Amber O'Neill,
special projects manager • Margot Wood, director of marketing & sales • Devin Funches,
sales & marketing manager • Katie Sainz, marketing manager • Tara Lehmann, publicist • Troy
Look, director of design & production • Kate Z. Stone, senior graphic designer • Sonja Synak,
graphic designer • Hilary Thompson, graphic designer • Sarah Rockwell, graphic designer
Angie Knowles, digital prepress lead • Vincent Kukua, digital prepress technician • Jasmine
Amiri, senior editor • Shawna Gore, senior editor • Amanda Meadows, senior editor • Robert
Meyers, senior editor, licensing • Desiree Rodriguez, editor • Grace Scheipeter, editor • Zack
Soto, editor • Chris Cerasi, editorial coordinator • Steve Ellis, vice president of games • Ben
Eisner, game developer • Michelle Nguyen, executive assistant • Jung Lee, logistics coordinator

Joe Nozemack, publisher emeritus

onipress.com
brennathummler.com /brennathummler

First Edition: March 2021

ISBN 978-1-62010-788-1
eISBN 978-1-62010-809-3

Printed in China.

Library of Congress Control Number: 2020937766
2 3 4 5 6 7 8 9 10